# MAKING MEMORIES

Adapted by Sarah Nathan

Based on the screenplay written by Peter Barsocchini

Based on characters created by Peter Barsocchini

Executive Producer Kenny Ortega

Produced by Bill Borden and Barry Rosenbush

Directed by Kenny Ortega

Copyright © 2008 Disney Enterprises, Inc.

All rights reserved. Published by Disney Press, an imprint of Disney Book Group. No part of this book may be reproduced or transmitted in any form or by any means, electronic or mechanical, including photocopying, recording, or by any information storage and retrieval system, without written permission from the publisher.

For information address Disney Press, 114 Fifth Avenue, New York, New York 10011-5690.

Printed in the United States of America

First Edition

1 3 5 7 9 10 8 6 4 2

Library of Congress Control Number: 2008904377

ISBN 978-1-4231-1204-4

For more Disney Press fun, visit www.disneybooks.com

Visit DisneyChannel.com/HighSchoolMusical

DISNEY PRESS

New York

The Wildcats have had so many wonderful experiences at East High! In good times and bad, the gang from East High have always been there for each other. Wildcats forever!

When Gabriella Montez and Troy Bolton met on New Year's Eve at the Sky Mountain Ski Resort, they had no idea where the night would take them. Once the music started, Gabriella and Troy could definitely tell it was the start of something new. And they were right. Gabriella would soon be a student at Troy's school!

Everyone was excited to be back at East High after the holiday break. Troy, who was captain of the Wildcats basketball team, was psyched for the upcoming championship game against their rivals, West High. "Wildcats! Get'cha head in the game!" Troy told his best friend, Chad Danforth, and the rest of his teammates.

Meanwhile, Taylor McKessie and the rest of the members of the Scholastic Decathlon really wanted to win their next competition. Taylor wanted Gabriella to be their newest member. She urged her to join, but Gabriella was hesitant.

Writing the new East High musical *Twinkle Towne* was like a dream come true for Kelsi Nielsen. And once she heard Troy and Gabriella sing, she knew they had to audition.

Troy and Gabriella really loved singing together, and decided to try out for the musical.

Sharpay Evans, diva of East High and the star of all the school's previous theater productions, couldn't believe that she had new competition. "Is this some kind of joke?" Sharpay fumed when she saw the callback sheet. Sharpay and her twin brother, Ryan, were *always* the leads!

When some of Troy's basketball teammates saw the callback sheet, they were shocked, too. Was Troy really going to try out for the winter musical? Taylor was just as surprised. Gabriella was supposed to focus on the upcoming Scholastic Decathlon competition.

Once word got out that Troy loved to sing, the Wildcats were buzzing about the news. "If Troy admits he sings," Zeke Baylor announced, "then I can tell my secret . . . I bake!" Suddenly, everyone was admitting what they secretly liked to do.

In the end, Troy's teammates and the members of the Scholastic Decathlon team supported Gabriella and Troy's decision to audition. As Troy and Gabriella sang together onstage, everyone knew that they were going to be chosen for the leads of *Twinkle Towne*.

It was a great day at East High. Not only did Gabriella and Troy get to audition, but the basketball team won the championship game, and the Scholastic Decathlon team defeated their competition! The Wildcats had learned that no matter what their interests, they were all in this together.

**W**hat time is it? Summer! When Sharpay overheard that Troy needed a summer job, she arranged for him to get one at the country club her family owned. Little did she know that Troy only agreed to the job if his friends could work there, too. "All for one and one for all!" Troy cheered.

Sharpay was determined to finally win over Troy and convince him to sing a duet with her at the country club's annual talent show. "It's out with the old and in with the new!" she exclaimed.

Kelsi's ears perked up when she heard about the talent show at the country club. She got to work on composing a song for Gabriella and Troy that she knew they would sing beautifully.

Gabriella was having fun being a lifeguard at the club pool, but she missed hanging out with Troy. When he got promoted and became a golf caddie, he was never around. To make things up to Gabriella, Troy planned a special picnic on the golf course.

When Sharpay found out that Ryan was helping the Wildcats with their routine for the talent show, she declared that no employees could be in the show. But Gabriella had enough of Sharpay's meddling. "It's our summer, remember?" she said to her friends. There was no way she was going to let Sharpay force them out of the show.

On the night of the talent show, Troy apologized to his friends for not being there for them. Then he told Sharpay that he'd do the show only if all the Wildcats performed with him. Sharpay knew that she had been defeated. "I sort of wish you were doing this for me," she told him. "You're a good guy, Troy." Sharpay knew he was making the right choice. And the talent show was still a huge success!

It's senior year! And that means the Wildcats were back on the basketball court. At the championship game, there were just seconds left on the clock. Troy passed the ball to sophomore Jimmie "The Rocket" Zara for the winning basket. The Wildcats won the championship two years in a row!

Ms. Darbus was happy about the Wildcats win, but even happier when she saw the sign-up sheet for the senior musical in homeroom the next morning. Kelsi had secretly signed up everyone to be part of the show! But the Wildcats weren't that excited. Luckily, Gabriella talked them into participating.

Now that basketball season was over, Troy was thinking of a way to ask Gabriella to the senior prom. He asked her to come up to the rooftop garden at school—their special place. "What I need is your help with an important decision," Troy said to her. He showed her a rack with a few tuxedos, and then he asked her which one she liked best. They danced around the rooftop in the rain. "Is that a yes?" Troy asked.

"In every language," Gabriella replied happily.